W9-AXP-708

The
Bear
on the
Bed

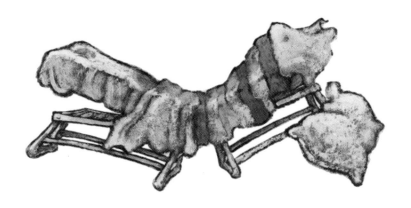

**To my father for his sense of humor —
and to the bear of course — R.M.**

**For Alan Graham, who has recently
bounced into my own life — B.S.**

Text © 2002 Ruth Miller
Illustrations © 2002 Bill Slavin

Kids Can Press acknowledges the financial support of the Ontario Arts Council,
the Canada Council for the Arts and the Government of Canada,
through the BPIDP, for our publishing activity.

Published in Canada by
Kids Can Press Ltd.
29 Birch Avenue
Toronto, ON M4V 1E2

Published in the U.S. by
Kids Can Press Ltd.
2250 Military Road
Tonawanda, NY 14150

www.kidscanpress.com

The artwork in this book was rendered in acrylics, on gessoed paper.
Text is set in Wilke Black.

Edited by Debbie Rogosin
Designed by Bill Slavin and Julia Naimska
Printed in Belgium by Proost NV

This book is smyth sewn casebound.

CM 02 0 9 8 7 6 5 4 3 2 1

National Library of Canada Cataloguing in Publication Data

Miller, Ruth, [date]
The bear on the bed

ISBN 1-55337-036-8

I. Slavin, Bill. II. Title.

PS8576.I5558B42 2002   jC813'.54   C2001-901517-8
PZ7.M633378Be 2002

E
292-8417

Kids Can Press is a Nelvana company

The Bear on the Bed

Written by
Ruth Miller

Illustrated by
Bill Slavin

Kids Can Press

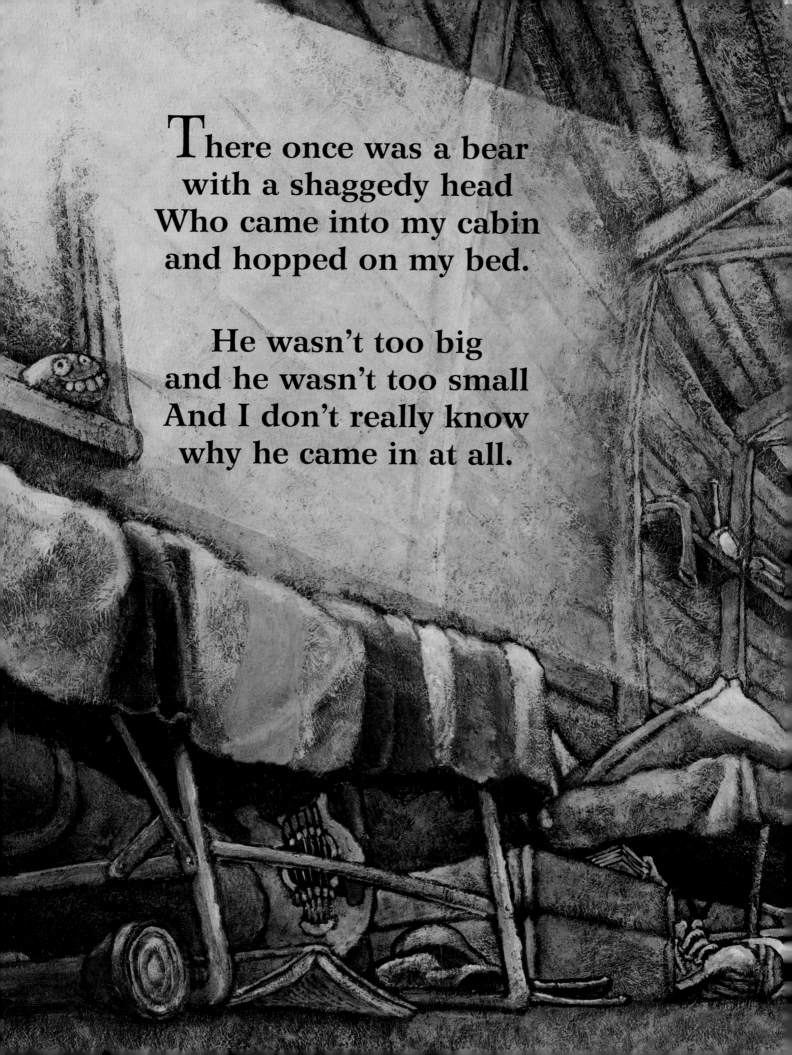

There once was a bear
with a shaggedy head
Who came into my cabin
and hopped on my bed.

He wasn't too big
and he wasn't too small
And I don't really know
why he came in at all.

He could have
played tennis
With Harry or

Dennis,

He could have gone jogging
With Lisa or Sue.

He could have gone fishing.
It's what I was wishing.
He could have gone sailing

Or *tipped* a canoe.

He could have,
he should have,
but guess what?
Instead ...

He settled
right down for
a snooze on
my bed.

He could have gone hiking,
He could have gone biking,

He could have
  gone swimming
Or high-diving,
 t o o.

He could have gone rowing —
Others were going.

He could have picked berries.
That's what bears do!

He could have,
he should have,
he didn't.
Instead ...
Plucking his
banjo,
he danced
on my bed.

He could have
done card tricks
Or played

p $_i$ c k- ^{u} p- s t $_i$ c k $_s$.

He could have made hot dogs
And marshmallow stew.

He could have played horseshoes.
That would have been good news.

He could have baked cookies
And eaten a few.

He could have,
he should have,
he didn't.
Instead ...
He jumped
up and down
and bounced
on my bed.

I wish that his sisters
And brothers had said,
"It isn't polite
To jump on a bed!"

I wish that his mama
And papa had said,
"Be careful, my precious,
you'll fall on your head!"

They could have, they should have, they didn't. Instead ...
He swung from the rafters over my bed.

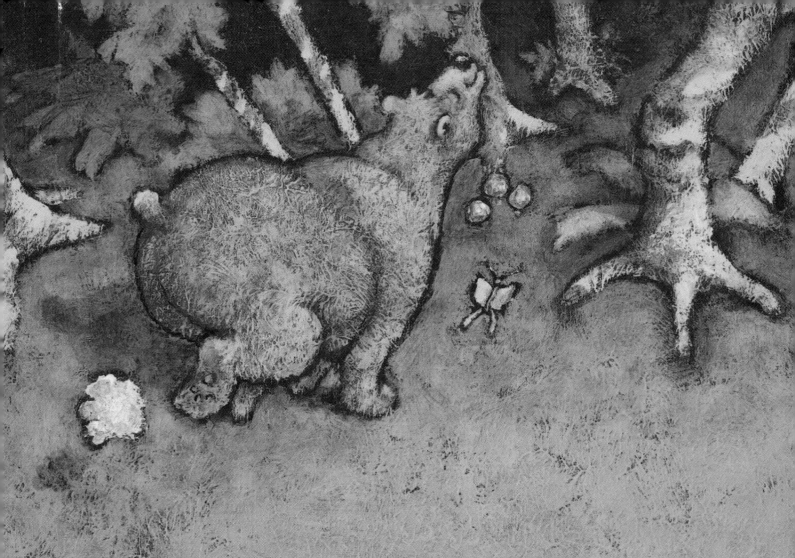

There once was a bear
with a shaggedy head
Who should have stayed far,
far away from my bed,

Who should have done something
quite other instead,
Like eating some jam
on a nice piece of bread.

But he couldn't, he wouldn't,
he didn't. Instead …
He came into my cabin
(now, I hope you'll believe me),
He just came right in
(you might not believe me),
He just waltzed right in
(oh please, please believe me)!

And after he snoozed
and danced on my bed,
And after he jumped
and bounced on my bed,
And after he almost fell
on his head ...

That naughty old bear ...